Second Chances... as a Grandparent

THIS TIME

Written by Keely R. Williams

Illustrated by Sue L. Perry

AUTHOR'S PAGE

THE DAY I BECAME A GRANDPARENT CHANGED MY LIFE FOR THE BETTER! I'VE BEEN ABLE TO REMINISCE ABOUT OUR CHILDREN'S CHILDHOOD AND ADJUST WAYS TO LOVE OUR NEWEST ADDITIONS! WE'RE CHOOSING TO SLOW DOWN, LAUGH MORE, AND INDULGE IN THE GIGGLES, MESSES AND SMILES!

DEDICATION

I DEDICATE MY FIRST CHILDREN'S BOOK TO OUR FIRST GRANDDAUGHTER, ELLIOT JANE DAVIS! I LOVE YOU TO THE MOON AND BACK AND ALL THE STARS IN BETWEEN. YOU'LL ALWAYS BE MY ELLIE BELLIE BOO, MY SILLY GOOSE AND MY VORACIOUS READER. I HOPE THIS WILL BE YOUR FAVORITE BOOK!!

It takes a lot to be a mommy and daddy, but **THIS TIME** we get a **Second Chance** to be a grandparent!

THIS TIME...

We'll hold you just a little bit longer...

and say our prayers to make you stronger.

THIS TIME...

we'll take more silly photos...

and track how much your body grows.

THIS TIME...

there will be more
giggles and laughs...

and we will pour more bubbles in the bath.

THIS TIME...

we'll make cookies
with sprinkles and
icing on cakes...

and have fancy picnics by the lake.

THIS TIME...

we'll read 3 books or more...

and build a blanket
tent on the floor.

THIS TIME...

life can slow down a bit...

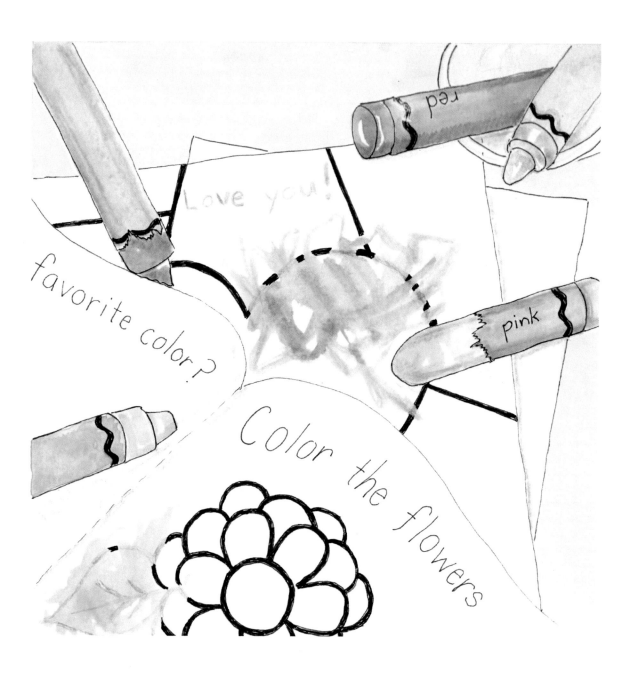

and we'll splurge with
a jumbo banana split.

THIS TIME...

we'll stop and smell the flowers...

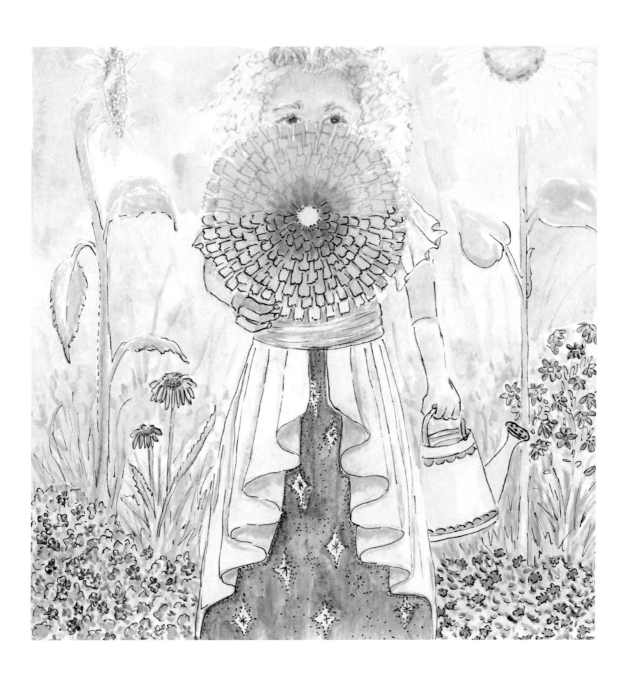

and splash puddles of water from the showers.

THIS TIME...

we'll pack bread to feed the ducks...

and play in the dirt
with dump trucks.

Mommy and daddy can be busy and that's why we're here... to make lots of memories year after year.

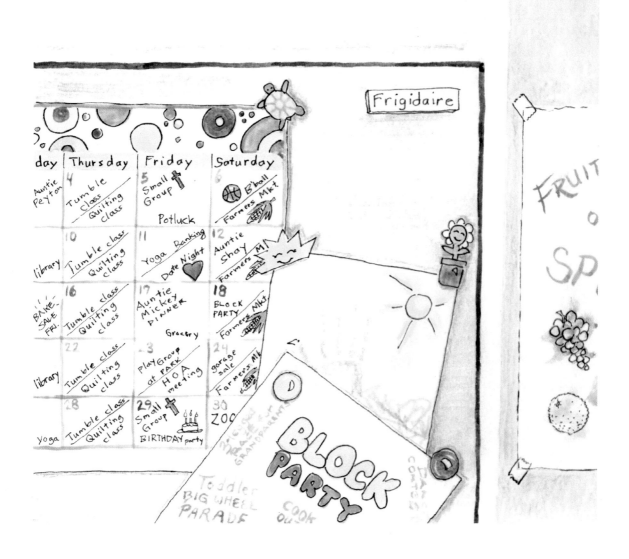

day	Thursday	Friday	Saturday
Auntie Peyton	4 Tumble Class Quilting class	5 Small Group Potluck	6 B'ball Farmers Mkt.
10 library	Tumble class Quilting class	11 Yoga Banking Date Night	12 Auntie Shay Farmers M!
16 BAKE-SALE FRI.	Tumble class Quilting class	17 Auntie Mickey DINNER Grocery	18 BLOCK PARTY Farmers Mkt
22 library	Tumble class Quilting class	23 Play Group at PARK H O A meeting	24 garage sale Farmers M!
28 yoga	Tumble class Quilting class	29 Small Group BIRTHDAY party	30 ZOO

Frigidaire

BLOCK PARTY

Toddler BIG WHEEL PARADE

COOK OUT

FRUIT o SP

Made in the USA
Las Vegas, NV
07 December 2024

13582070R00024